The Watsons

Jane Austen

ET REMOTISSIMA PROPE

Hesperus Classics

Hesperus Classics
Published by Hesperus Press Limited
4 Rickett Street, London SW6 1RU
www.hesperuspress.com

First published in *A Memoir of Jane Austen* by James Edward Austen-Leigh, 1870
First published by Hesperus Press Limited, 2007

Designed and typeset by Fraser Muggeridge studio
Printed in Jordan by Jordan National Press

ISBN: 1-84391-145-0
ISBN13: 978-1-84391-145-6

CONTENTS

FOREWORD

The fragment that is *The Watsons* stands in an interesting position in Jane Austen's canon. When she began it in 1804 she already had three novels to her name – *Susan*, *Elinor and Marianne* and *First Impressions*. *Elinor and Marianne*, written originally in epistolary form, would become *Sense and Sensibility* and eventually be published in 1811. *First Impressions* had already been offered to a publisher in 1797 and rejected unseen. Redrafted (famously 'lop't and crop't', in Jane Austen's own words) it was finally published in 1813 as *Pride and Prejudice*. Despite its initial rejection, Austen seems to have retained a sense of authorial confidence in *First Impressions* – we know it was a favourite within her family – and when the manuscript of *Susan* was accepted by Crosby and Company in 1803 it might have seemed to Jane Austen that she was a young woman on the cusp of her own brilliant career.

However Austen never saw *Susan* published in her lifetime. The brilliant career was unexpectedly stalled and in the decade up to 1809 the only thing that Jane Austen wrote was *The Watsons*.

There are conflicting opinions about this period of drought in Austen's literary life. Certainly they were trying times for her, characterised by upheaval, heartache and death. In 1800 her parents had made the sudden decision to retire to Bath and Cassandra and Jane were precipitously uprooted from the rural familiarity of the Steventon parsonage, the only home they had ever known. Early in 1805 Mr Austen died, leaving his wife and daughters dependent on the Austen brothers for their financial security. The letters from this period are missing – none at all between May 1801 and September 1804 – destroyed by Cassandra, no doubt out of loyalty. Austen could be caustic and bitter: well and good in the intimacy of a letter to a sister, but not necessarily remarks meant for public consumption.

It was only in 1809 that Jane, Cassandra and their mother settled again for good in Chawton and Jane recommenced writing.

Thus are the bare bones of the plot: at an early age, Emma Watson was adopted by an apparently loving aunt and uncle and brought up with the expectation of inheriting a fortune from them. The uncle, however, has recently died without making provision in his will for Emma, trusting his widow to do so. She, however, has married a fortune hunter who wishes to have nothing more to do with Emma who has been summarily returned to the chilly bosom of a family she hardly knows. Or, as her brother, Robert, puts it more brutally, 'Instead of heiress of 8,000 or 9,000 l., [you are] sent back a weight upon your family, without a sixpence.'

Like Jane Austen's own father, Emma's father is a retired clergyman, a frail, weak invalid near to death. It was shortly after her father's death (following closely on the death of her friend Mrs Lefroy) that Jane Austen abandoned writing *The Watsons*, and it is not wild conjecture to think that it was too painful for her to have carried on with this strand of the plot. Death is rarely, if ever, essayed in Austen's work, although in the letters she is pragmatic to the point of callousness – perhaps a good defence at a time when death was a commonplace.

The Watsons live a quiet provincial life in Stanton (on the most literal level, notice how many letters it shares with the lost Steventon). Stanton seems agreeably dull, a place where after the excitement of dancing one can look forward to 'some comfortable soup', a place where the 'great wash' occupies a good deal of energy and people can make an unfashionably early supper from fried beef. Stanton certainly seems to have a more congenial character than most of the people who populate it: never in an Austen novel have so many unpleasant people rushed to make our acquaintance so quickly. True, there are the Edwards and Mr Howard and his sister, perfectly good and kind, but the Osbornes, the local gentry, are ill-mannered and self-obsessed. 'The Osbornes are to be no rule for us', Mr Edwards says sensibly, and one suspects Austen planned some energetic conflicts between provincial manners and aristocratic pretensions. Then there is Tom Musgrave, with whom Emma's sister, Margaret, is embarrassingly smitten. He is attractive and charming and therefore we can be sure he is damned in the manner of a Henry Crawford or a Willoughby. And last but not least there are Emma's siblings, who display 'hard-hearted prosperity, low-minded conceit, and wrong-headed folly, engrafted on an untoward disposition'. No saving virtues there it seems!

Emma's sisters, Elizabeth, Margaret and Penelope, are consumed by the desperate hunt for a husband. They have, of course, little choice, for when Mr Watson dies they will be dependent on the charity of their unpleasant brother Robert and his equally unpleasant wife. 'We must marry,' Elizabeth declares to Emma, '…it is very bad to grow old and be poor and laughed at.' (One thinks of Charlotte Lucas settling for Mr Collins as a way of avoiding this fate.) But, of course, what Austen says to us at every turn in her work is that one *does* have a choice. All of her heroines put their own integrity ahead of the imperative of marriage; indeed Elizabeth Bennet refuses the greatest match of them all the first time round.

Elizabeth Watson's viewpoint is unacceptable to her sister, Emma, who declares, 'Poverty is a great evil, but to a woman of education and feeling it ought not, it cannot be the greatest.'

The newcomer is always a novelty in a small society and Emma Watson is no exception. 'Many were the eyes, and various the degrees of approbation with which she was examined', Austen writes – a sentence that carries an extraordinary burden of passivity. Emma's prospective passage through the novel will be that of other Austen heroines (with the exception of Emma Woodhouse, Austen's only prosperous protagonist) in that she must learn to live within the constraints of her situation and yet achieve the results she desires.

The reward for the Austen heroine who retains her principles in the face of social dicta is of course, ironically, a good marriage, based on love and, at the very least, a decent measure of financial security. This was to be the fate of Emma Watson, who, according to Cassandra, Austen intended to marry to the clergyman, Mr Howard. She was also to be pursued by the arrogant Lord Osborne with whom she has some robust exchanges of opinion ('Female economy will do a great deal my lord: but it cannot turn a small income into a large one'). Money, and the female lack of it, informs every turn of the text.

Emma Watson has wit and spirit and she is certainly possessed of a good nature, as we see in the most charming scene in the book when she dances with the mortified young Charles Blake after he is let down by Lord Osborne's selfish sister at the great set piece of the local assembly dance. Yet Emma Watson does not quite have the sparkle of Elizabeth Bennet or the exuberance of her namesake-to-be Emma Woodhouse, and it seems unlikely that she will be tested emotionally to the degree that Elinor and Marianne Dashwood are (although surely no one has ever suffered more silently in a novel than Anne Eliot). The main 'problem' with Emma Watson, however, is that she comes to us fully formed, already having suffered the worst of rejections and disappointments – 'My conduct must tell you how I have been brought up… if my opinions are wrong, I must correct them.' How unlike the *other* Emma's journey of self-learning or Elizabeth Bennet's sudden shocking awareness of her wrong-thinking.

There are certainly flaws in *The Watsons*: the somewhat fixed characters of the protagonists, more black and white than light and shade, and the rather heavy-handed opening in which Elizabeth plays extensive catch-up with Emma in a tell-not-show way that is uncharacteristic of Austen's deftness. There is undoubtedly a bleakness at the heart of *The Watsons* – in some ways the plot is a dark version of *First Impressions* – but there are delights along the way, not least in the perfectly turned satire of the authorial voice – before being able to set off to the ball from the Edwards' house Emma has to brave 'a great deal of indifferent cooking and anxious suspense'.

Like most women of her time Jane Austen had little control over her circumstances, a plight that is at the heart of *The Watsons*, as it is in all her novels. It is hardly a surprise that so many women turned to writing fiction in the nineteenth century, for a writer can order her own world, the world of the novel, exactly how she pleases.

The Watsons, the text that gives a voice to the silence of those restless years, is in some instances uncomfortably close to the life that was being lived, or in some cases, no doubt, endured.

– Kate Atkinson, 2007

The Watsons

The first winter assembly in the town of D— in Surrey was to be held on Tuesday, 13th October and it was generally expected to be a very good one. A long list of county families was confidently run over as sure of attending, and sanguine hopes were entertained that the Osbornes themselves would be there. The Edwards' invitation to the Watsons followed, of course. The Edwards were people of fortune, who lived in the town and kept their coach. The Watsons inhabited a village about three miles distant, were poor, and had no close carriage, and ever since there had been balls in the place, the former were accustomed to invite the latter to dress, dine, and sleep at their house on every monthly return throughout the winter. On the present occasion, as only two of Mr Watson's children were at home, and one was always necessary as companion to himself, for he was sickly and had lost his wife, one only could profit by the kindness of their friends. Miss Emma Watson, who was very recently returned to her family from the care of an aunt who had brought her up, was to make her first public appearance in the neighbourhood, and her eldest sister, whose delight in a ball was not lessened by a ten years' enjoyment, had some merit in cheerfully undertaking to drive her and all her finery in the old chair to D— on the important morning.

As they splashed along the dirty lane, Miss Watson thus instructed and cautioned her inexperienced sister –

'I dare say it will be a very good ball, and among so many officers you will hardly want partners. You will find Mrs Edwards' maid very willing to help you, and I would advise you to ask Mary Edwards' opinion if you are at all at a loss, for she has a very good taste. If Mr Edwards does not lose his money at cards, you will stay as late as you can wish for; if he does, he will hurry you home perhaps – but you are sure of some comfortable soup. I hope you will be in good looks. I should not be surprised if you were to be thought one of the prettiest girls in the room; there is a great deal in novelty. Perhaps Tom Musgrave may take notice of you, but I would advise you by all means not to give him any encouragement. He generally pays attention to every new girl, but he is a great flirt, and never means anything serious.'

'I think I have heard you speak of him before,' said Emma; 'who is he?'

'A young man of very good fortune, quite independent, and remarkably agreeable – a universal favourite wherever he goes. Most of the girls hereabout are in love with him, or have been. I believe I am the only one among them that have escaped with a whole heart, and yet I was the first he paid attention to when he came into this country six years ago, and very great attention did he pay me. Some people say that he has never seemed to like any girl so well since, though he is always behaving in a particular way to one or another.'

'And how came *your* heart to be the only cold one?' said Emma, smiling.

'There was a reason for that,' replied Miss Watson, changing colour – 'I have not been very well used among them, Emma. I hope you will have better luck.'

'Dear sister, I beg your pardon if I have unthinkingly given you pain.'

'When first we knew Tom Musgrave,' continued Miss Watson, without seeming to hear her, 'I was very much attached to a young man of the name of Purvis, a particular friend of Robert's, who used to be with us a great deal. Everybody thought it would have been a match.'

A sigh accompanied these words, which Emma respected in silence, but her sister after a short pause went on.

'You will naturally ask why it did not take place, and why he is married to another woman, while I am still single. But you must ask her, not me – you must ask Penelope. Yes, Emma, Penelope was at the bottom of it all. She thinks everything fair for a husband. I trusted her; she set him against me, with a view of gaining him herself, and it ended in his discontinuing his visits, and soon after marrying somebody else. Penelope makes light of her conduct, but *I* think such treachery very bad. It has been the ruin of my happiness. I shall never love any man as I loved Purvis. I do not think Tom Musgrave should be named with him in the same day.'

'You quite shock me by what you say of Penelope,' said Emma. 'Could a sister do such a thing? Rivalry, treachery between sisters! I shall be afraid of being acquainted with her. But I hope it was not so; appearances were against her.'

'You do not know Penelope. There is nothing she would not do to get married. She would as good as tell you so herself. Do not trust her with any secrets of your own, take warning by me, do not trust her; she has her good qualities, but she has no faith, no honour, no scruples, if she can promote her own advantage. I wish with all my heart she was well married. I declare I had rather have her well married than myself.'

'Than yourself! yes, I can suppose so. A heart wounded like yours can have little inclination for matrimony.'

'Not much indeed – but you know we must marry. I could do very well single for my own part; a little company, and a pleasant ball now and then, would be enough for me, if one could be young forever, but my father cannot provide for us, and it is very bad to grow old and be poor and laughed at. I have lost Purvis, it is true, but very few people marry their first loves. I should not refuse a man because he was not Purvis. Not that I can ever quite forgive Penelope.'

Emma shook her head in acquiescence.

'Penelope, however, has had her troubles,' continued Miss Watson. 'She was sadly disappointed in Tom Musgrave, who afterwards transferred his attentions from me to her, and whom she was very fond of, but he never means anything serious, and when he had trifled with her long enough, he began to slight her for Margaret, and poor Penelope was very wretched. And since then she has been trying to make some match at Chichester – she won't tell us with whom, but I believe it is a rich old Dr Harding, uncle to the friend she goes to see, and she has taken a vast deal of trouble about him, and given up a great deal of time to no purpose as yet. When she went away the other day, she said it should be the last time. I suppose you did not know what her particular business was at Chichester, nor guess at the object that could take her away from Stanton just as you were coming home after so many years' absence.'

'No indeed, I had not the smallest suspicion of it. I considered her engagement to Mrs Shaw just at that time as very unfortunate for me. I had hoped to find all my sisters at home, to be able to make an immediate friend of each.'

'I suspect the Doctor to have had an attack of the asthma, and that she was hurried away on that account. The Shaws are quite on her side – at least, I believe so, but she tells me nothing. She professes to keep her own counsel; she says, and truly enough, that "Too many cooks spoil the broth."'

'I am sorry for her anxieties,' said Emma, 'but I do not like her plans or her opinions. I shall be afraid of her. She must have too masculine and bold a temper. To be so bent on marriage, to pursue a man merely for the sake of situation, is a sort of thing that shocks me; I cannot understand it. Poverty is a great evil, but to a woman of education and feeling it ought not, it cannot be the greatest. I would rather be teacher at a school (and I can think of nothing worse) than marry a man I did not like.'

'I would rather do anything than be teacher at a school,' said her sister. '*I* have been at school, Emma, and know what a life they lead; *you* never have. I should not like marrying a disagreeable man any more than yourself, but I do not think there *are* many very disagreeable men; I think I could like any good-humoured man with a comfortable income. I suppose my aunt brought you up to be rather refined.'

'Indeed I do not know. My conduct must tell you how I have been brought up. I am no judge of it myself. I cannot compare my aunt's method with any other person's, because I know no other.'

'But I can see in a great many things that you are very refined. I have observed it ever since you came home, and I am afraid it will not be for your happiness. Penelope will laugh at you very much.'

'*That* will not be for my happiness, I an sure. If my opinions are wrong, I must correct them; if they are above my situation, I must endeavour to conceal them; but I doubt whether ridicule – has Penelope much wit?'

'Yes; she has great spirits, and never cares what she says.'

'Margaret is more gentle, I imagine?'

'Yes; especially in company. She is all gentleness and mildness when anybody is by, but she is a little fretful and perverse among ourselves. Poor creature! She is possessed with the notion of Tom Musgrave's being more seriously in love with her than he ever was with anybody else, and is always expecting him to come to the point. This is the second time within this twelvemonth that she has gone to spend a month with Robert and Jane on purpose to egg him on by her absence, but

I am sure she is mistaken, and that he will no more follow her to Croydon now than he did last March. He will never marry unless he can marry somebody very great – Miss Osborne, perhaps, or something in that style.'

'Your account of this Tom Musgrave, Elizabeth, gives me very little inclination for his acquaintance.'

'You are afraid of him; I do not wonder at you.'

'No, indeed; I dislike and despise him.'

'Dislike and despise Tom Musgrave! No, *that* you never can. I defy you not to be delighted with him if he takes notice of you. I hope he will dance with you; and I dare say he will, unless the Osbornes come with a large party, and then he will not speak to anybody else.'

'He seems to have most engaging manners!' said Emma. 'Well, we shall see how irresistible Mr Tom Musgrave and I find each other. I suppose I shall know him as soon as I enter the ballroom; he *must* carry some of his charm in his face.'

'You will not find him in the ballroom, I can tell you; you will go early, that Mrs Edwards may get a good place by the fire, and he never comes till late; if the Osbornes are coming, he will wait in the passage and come in with them. I should like to look in upon you, Emma. If it was but a good day with my father, I would wrap myself up, and James should drive me over as soon as I had made tea for him, and I should be with you by the time the dancing began.'

'What! Would you come late at night in this chair?'

'To be sure I would. There, I said you were very refined, and *that*'s an instance of it.'

Emma for a moment made no answer. At last she said –

'I wish, Elizabeth, you had not made a point of my going to this ball; I wish you were going instead of me. Your pleasure would be greater than mine. I am a stranger here, and know nobody but the Edwardses; my enjoyment, therefore, must be very doubtful. Yours, among all your acquaintance, would be certain. It is not too late to change. Very little apology could be requisite to the Edwardses, who must be more glad of your company than of mine, and I should most readily return to my father, and should not be at all afraid to drive this quiet old creature home. Your clothes I would undertake to find means of sending to you.'

'My dearest Emma,' cried Elizabeth, warmly, 'do you think I would do such a thing? Not for the universe! But I shall never forget your good nature in proposing it. You must have a sweet temper indeed! I never met with anything like it! And would you really give up the ball that I might be able to go to it? Believe me, Emma, I am not so selfish as that comes to. No; though I am nine years older than you are, I would not be the means of keeping you from being seen. You are very pretty, and it would be very hard that you should not have as fair a chance as we have all had to make your fortune. No, Emma, whoever stays at home this winter, it shan't be you. I am sure I should never have forgiven the person who kept me from a ball at nineteen.'

Emma expressed her gratitude, and for a few minutes they jogged on in silence. Elizabeth first spoke –

'You will take notice who Mary Edwards dances with?'

'I will remember her partners, if I can, but you know they will be all strangers to me.'

'Only observe whether she dances with Captain Hunter more than once – I have my fears in that quarter. Not that her father or mother like officers, but if she does, you know, it is all over with poor Sam. And I have promised to write him word who she dances with.'

'Is Sam attached to Miss Edwards?'

'Did not you know *that*?'

'How should I know it? How should I know in Shropshire what is passing of that nature in Surrey? It is not likely that circumstances of such delicacy should have made any part of the scanty communication that passed between you and me for the last fourteen years.'

'I wonder I never mentioned it when I wrote. Since you have been at home, I have been so busy with my poor father and our great wash that I have had no leisure to tell you anything, but, indeed, I concluded you knew it all. He has been very much in love with her these two years, and it is a great disappointment to him that he cannot always get away to our balls, but Mr Curtis won't often spare him, and just now it is a sickly time at Guildford.'

'Do you suppose Miss Edwards inclined to like him?'

'I am afraid not: you know she is an only child, and will have at least ten thousand pounds.'

'But still she may like our brother.'

'Oh, no! The Edwards look much higher. Her father and mother would never consent to it. Sam is only a surgeon, you know. Sometimes I think she does like him. But Mary Edwards is rather prim and reserved; I do not always know what she would be at.'

'Unless Sam feels on sure grounds with the lady herself, it seems a pity to me that he should be encouraged to think of her at all.'

'A young man must think of somebody,' said Elizabeth, 'and why should not he be as lucky as Robert, who has got a good wife and six thousand pounds?'

'We must not all expect to be individually lucky,' replied Emma. 'The luck of one member of a family is luck to all.'

'Mine is all to come, I am sure,' said Elizabeth, giving another sigh to the remembrance of Purvis. 'I have been unlucky enough, and I cannot say much for you, as my aunt married again so foolishly. Well, you will have a good ball, I dare say. The next turning will bring us to the turnpike: you may see the church tower over the hedge, and the White Hart is close by it. I shall long to know what you think of Tom Musgrave.'

Such were the last audible sounds of Miss Watson's voice, before they passed through the turnpike gate, and entered on the pitching of the town, the jumbling and noise of which made further conversation most thoroughly undesirable. The old mare trotted heavily on, wanting no direction of the reins to take the right turning, and making only one blunder, in proposing to stop at the milliner's before she drew up towards Mr Edwards' door. Mr Edwards lived in the best house in the street, and the best in the place, if Mr Tomlinson, the banker, might be indulged in calling his newly erected house at the end of the town, with a shrubbery and sweep, in the country.

Mr Edwards' house was higher than most of its neighbours, with four windows on each side of the door, the windows guarded by posts and chains, and the door approached by a flight of stone steps.

'Here we are,' said Elizabeth, as the carriage ceased moving, 'safely arrived, and by the market clock we have been only five-and-thirty minutes coming, which *I* think is doing pretty well, though it would be nothing for Penelope. Is not it a nice town? The Edwards have a noble house, you see, and they live quite in style. The door will be opened by a man in livery, with a powdered head, I can tell you.'

Emma had seen the Edwardses only one morning at Stanton; they were therefore all but strangers to her, and though her spirits were by no means insensible to the expected joys of the evening, she felt a little uncomfortable in the thought of all that was to precede them. Her conversation with Elizabeth, too, giving her some very unpleasant feelings with respect to her own family, had made her more open to disagreeable impressions from any other cause, and increased her sense of the awkwardness of rushing into intimacy on so slight an acquaintance.

There was nothing in the manner of Mrs or Miss Edwards to give immediate change to these ideas. The mother, though a very friendly woman, had a reserved air, and a great deal of formal civility, and the daughter, a genteel-looking girl of twenty-two, with her hair in papers, seemed very naturally to have caught something of the style of her mother, who had brought her up. Emma was soon left to know what they could be, by Elizabeth's being obliged to hurry away, and some very languid remarks on the probable brilliancy of the ball were all that broke, at intervals, a silence of half an hour, before they were joined by the master of the house. Mr Edwards had a much easier and more communicative air than the ladies of the family; he was fresh from the street, and he came ready to tell whatever might interest. After a cordial reception of Emma, he turned to his daughter with –

'Well, Mary, I bring you good news: the Osbornes will certainly be at the ball tonight. Horses for two carriages are ordered from the White Hart to be at Osborne Castle by nine.'

'I am glad of it,' observed Mrs Edwards, 'because their coming gives a credit to our assembly. The Osbornes being known to have been at the first ball, will dispose a great many people to attend the second. It is more than they deserve, for in fact, they add nothing to the pleasure of the evening: they come so late and go so early; but great people have always their charm.'

Mr Edwards proceeded to relate every other little article of news that his morning's lounge had supplied him with, and they chatted with greater briskness, till Mrs Edwards' moment for dressing arrived, and the young ladies were carefully recommended to lose no time. Emma was shown to a very comfortable apartment, and as soon as Mrs Edwards' civilities could leave her to herself, the happy occupation, the first bliss of a ball, began. The girls, dressing in some measure together, grew unavoidably better acquainted. Emma found in Miss Edwards the show of good sense, a modest unpretending mind, and a great wish of obliging, and when they returned to the parlour where Mrs Edwards was sitting, respectably attired in one of the two satin gowns that went through the winter, and a new cap from the milliner's, they entered it with much easier feelings and more natural smiles than they had taken away. Their dress was now to be examined: Mrs Edwards acknowledged herself too old-fashioned to approve of every modern extravagance, however sanctioned, and though complacently viewing her daughter's good looks, would give but a qualified admiration, and Mr Edwards, not less satisfied with Mary, paid some compliments of good-humoured gallantry to Emma at her expense. The discussion led to more intimate remarks, and Miss Edwards gently asked Emma if she were not often reckoned very like her youngest brother. Emma thought she could perceive a faint blush accompany the question, and there seemed something still more suspicious in the manner in which Mr Edwards took up the subject.

'You are paying Miss Emma no great compliment, I think, Mary,' said he, hastily. 'Mr Sam Watson is a very good sort of young man, and I dare say a very clever surgeon, but his complexion has been rather too much exposed to all weathers to make a likeness to him very flattering.'

Mary apologised, in some confusion –

'She had not thought a strong likeness at all incompatible with very different degrees of beauty. There might be resemblance in countenance, and the complexion and even the features be very unlike.'

'I know nothing of my brother's beauty,' said Emma, 'for I have not seen him since he was seven years old, but my father reckons us alike.'

'Mr Watson!' cried Mr Edwards; 'well, you astonish me. There is not the least likeness in the world; your brother's eyes are grey, yours are brown; he has a long face and a wide mouth. My dear, do *you* perceive the least resemblance?'

'Not the least. Miss Emma Watson puts me very much in mind of her eldest sister, and sometimes I see a look of Miss Penelope, and once or twice there has been a glance of Mr Robert, but I cannot perceive any likeness to Mr Samuel.'

'I see the likeness between her and Miss Watson,' replied Mr Edwards, 'very strongly, but I am not sensible of the others. I do not much think she is like any of the family *but* Miss Watson, but I am very sure there is no resemblance between her and Sam.'

This matter was settled, and they went to dinner.

'Your father, Miss Emma, is one of my oldest friends,' said Mr Edwards, as he helped her to wine, when they were drawn round the fire to enjoy their dessert. 'We must drink to his better health. It is a great concern to me, I assure you, that he should be such an invalid. I know nobody who likes a game of cards, in a social way, better than he does, and very few people that play a fairer rubber. It is a thousand pities that he should be so deprived of the pleasure. For now we have a quiet little whist club, which meets three times a week at the White Hart, and if he could but have his health, how much he would enjoy it!'

'I dare say he would, sir, and I wish, with all my heart, he were equal to it.'

'Your club would be better fitted for an invalid,' said Mrs Edwards, 'if you did not keep it up so late.'

This was an old grievance.

'So late, my dear! What are you talking of?' cried the husband, with sturdy pleasantry. 'We are always at home before midnight. They would laugh at Osborne Castle to hear you call *that* late; they are but just rising from dinner at midnight.'

'That is nothing to the purpose,' retorted the lady, calmly. 'The Osbornes are to be no rule for us. You had better meet every night, and break up two hours sooner.'

So far the subject was very often carried, but Mr and Mrs Edwards were so wise as never to pass that point, and Mr Edwards now turned to something else. He had lived long enough in the idleness of a town to become a little of a gossip, and having some anxiety to know more of the circumstances of his young guest than had yet reached him, he began with –

'I think, Miss Emma, I remember your aunt very well, about thirty years ago; I am pretty sure I danced with her in the old rooms at Bath, the year before I married. She was a very fine woman then, but like other people, I suppose, she is grown somewhat older since that time. I hope she is likely to be happy in her second choice.'

'I hope so; I believe so, sir,' said Emma, in some agitation.

'Mr Turner had not been dead a great while, I think?'

'About two years, sir.'

'I forget what her name is now.'

'O'Brien.'

'Irish! ah, I remember; and she is gone to settle in Ireland. I do wonder that you should not wish to go with her into *that* country, Miss Emma, but it must be a great deprivation to her, poor lady! after bringing you up like a child of her own.'

'I was not so ungrateful, sir,' said Emma, warmly, 'as to wish to be anywhere but with her. It did not suit them, it did not suit Captain O'Brien that I should be of the party.'

'Captain!' repeated Mrs Edwards. 'The gentleman is in the army then?'

'Yes, ma'am.'

'Aye, there is nothing like your officers for captivating the ladies, young or old. There is no resisting a cockade, my dear.'

'I hope there is,' said Mrs Edwards, gravely, with a quick glance at her daughter, and Emma had just recovered from her own perturbation in time to see a blush on Miss Edwards' cheek, and in remembering what Elizabeth had said of Captain Hunter, to wonder and waver between his influence and her brother's.

'Elderly ladies should be careful how they make a second choice,' observed Mr Edwards.

'Carefulness – discretion should not be confined to elderly ladies or to a second choice,' added his wife. 'They are quite as necessary to young ladies in their first.'

'Rather more so, my dear,' replied he, 'because young ladies are likely to feel the effects of it longer. When an old lady plays the fool, it is not in the course of nature that she should suffer from it many years.'

Emma drew her hand across her eyes, and Mrs Edwards, on perceiving it, changed the subject to one of less anxiety to all.

With nothing to do but to expect the hour of setting off, the afternoon was long to the two young ladies, and though Miss Edwards was rather discomposed at the very early hour that her mother always fixed for going, that early hour itself was watched for with some eagerness.

The entrance of the tea-things at seven o'clock was some relief, and luckily Mr and Mrs Edwards always drank a dish extraordinary and ate an additional muffin when they were going to sit up late, which lengthened the ceremony almost to the wished-for moment.

At a little before eight, the Tomlinsons' carriage was heard to go by – which was the constant signal for Mrs Edwards to order hers to the door, and in a very few minutes the party were transported from the quiet and warmth of a snug parlour to the bustle, noise, and draughts of air of the broad entrance passage of an inn. Mrs Edwards, carefully guarding her own dress, while she attended with yet greater solicitude to the proper security of her young charges' shoulders and throats, led the way up the wide staircase, while no sound of a ball but the first scrape of one violin blessed the ears of her followers, and Miss Edwards, on hazarding the anxious enquiry of whether there were many people come yet, was told by the waiter, as she knew she should, that 'Mr Tomlinson's family were in the room.'

In passing along a short gallery to the assembly room, brilliant in lights before them, they were accosted by a young man in a morning dress and boots, who was standing in the doorway of a bedchamber, apparently on purpose to see them go by.

'Ah! Mrs Edwards, how do you do? How do you do, Miss Edwards?' he cried, with an easy air. 'You are determined to be in good time, I see, as usual. The candles are but this moment lit.'

'I like to get a good seat by the fire, you know, Mr Musgrave,' replied Mrs Edwards.

'I am this moment going to dress,' said he. 'I am waiting for my stupid fellow. We shall have a famous ball. The Osbornes are certainly coming; you may depend upon *that*, for I was with Lord Osborne this morning.'

The party passed on. Mrs Edwards' satin gown swept along the clean floor of the ballroom to the fireplace at the upper end, where one party only were formally seated, while three or four officers were lounging together, passing in and out from the adjoining card room. A very stiff meeting between these near neighbours ensued, and as soon as they were all duly placed again, Emma, in the low whisper that became the solemn scene, said to Miss Edwards –

'The gentleman we passed in the passage was Mr Musgrave, then; he is reckoned remarkably agreeable, I understand?'

Miss Edwards answered hesitatingly, 'Yes; he is very much liked by many people, but *we* are not very intimate.'

'He is rich, is not he?'

'He has about eight or nine hundred pounds a year, I believe. He came into possession of it when he was very young, and my father and mother think it has given him rather an unsettled turn. He is no favourite with them.'

The cold and empty appearance of the room and the demure air of the small cluster of females at one end of it, began soon to give way. The inspiriting sound of other carriages was heard, and continual accessions of portly chaperons and strings of smartly dressed girls were received, with now and then a fresh gentleman straggler, who, if not enough in love to station himself near any fair creature, seemed glad to escape into the card room.

Among the increasing number of military men, one now made his way to Miss Edwards with an air of *empressement* that decidedly said to her companion, 'I am Captain Hunter', and Emma, who could not but watch her at such a moment, saw her looking rather distressed, but by no means displeased, and heard an engagement formed for the two first dances, which made her think her brother Sam's a hopeless case.

Emma in the meanwhile was not unobserved or unadmired herself. A new face, and a very pretty one, could not be slighted. Her name was whispered from one party to another, and no sooner had the signal been given by the orchestra's striking up a favourite air, which seemed to call the young to their duty and people the centre of the room, than she found herself engaged to dance with a brother officer, introduced by Captain Hunter.

Emma Watson was not more than of the middle height, well made and plump, with an air of healthy vigour. Her skin was very brown, but clear, smooth, and glowing, which, with a lively eye, a sweet smile, and an open countenance, gave beauty to attract, and expression to make that beauty improve on acquaintance. Having no reason to be dissatisfied with her partner, the evening began very pleasantly to her, and her feelings perfectly coincided with the reiterated observation of others, that it was an excellent ball. The two first dances were not quite over when the returning sound of carriages after a long interruption called general notice, and 'The Osbornes are coming! The Osbornes are coming!' was repeated round the room. After some minutes of extraordinary bustle without and watchful curiosity within, the important party, preceded by the attentive master of the inn to open a door that was never shut, made their appearance. They consisted of Lady Osborne; her son, Lord Osborne; her daughter, Miss Osborne; Miss Carr, her daughter's friend; Mr Howard, formerly tutor to Lord Osborne, now clergyman of the parish in which the castle stood; Mrs Blake, a widow sister who lived with him; her son, a fine boy of ten years old; and Mr Tom Musgrave, who probably, imprisoned within his own room, had been listening in bitter impatience to the sound of the music for the last half-hour. In their progress up the room, they paused almost immediately behind Emma to receive the compliments of some acquaintance, and she heard Lady Osborne observe that they had made a point of coming early for the gratification of Mrs Blake's little boy, who was uncommonly fond of dancing. Emma looked at them all as they passed, but chiefly and with most interest on Tom Musgrave, who was certainly a genteel, good-looking young man. Of the females, Lady Osborne had by much the finest person; though nearly fifty, she was very handsome, and had all the dignity of rank.

Lord Osborne was a very fine young man, but there was an air of coldness, of carelessness, even of awkwardness about him, which seemed to speak him out of his element in a ball-room. He came, in fact, only because it was judged expedient for him to please the borough; he was not fond of women's company, and he never danced. Mr Howard was an agreeable-looking man, a little more than thirty.

At the conclusion of the two dances, Emma found herself, she knew not how, seated amongst the Osborne set, and she was immediately struck with the fine countenance and anim-ated gestures of the little boy, as he was standing before his mother, wondering when they should begin.

'You will not be surprised at Charles' impatience,' said Mrs Blake, a lively, pleasant-looking little woman of five- or six-and-thirty, to a lady who was standing near her, 'when you know what a partner he is to have. Miss Osborne has been so very kind as to promise to dance the two first dances with him.'

'Oh, yes! we have been engaged this week,' cried the boy, 'and we are to dance down every couple.'

On the other side of Emma, Miss Osborne, Miss Carr, and a party of young men were standing engaged in very lively consultation, and soon afterwards she saw the smartest officer of the set walking off to the orchestra to order the dance, while Miss Osborne, passing before her to her little expecting partner, hastily said: 'Charles, I beg your pardon for not keeping my engagement, but I am going to dance these two dances with Colonel Beresford. I know you will excuse me, and I will certainly dance with you after tea'; and without staying for an answer, she turned again to Miss Carr, and in another minute was led by Colonel Beresford to begin the set. If the poor little boy's face had in its happiness been interesting to Emma, it was infinitely more so under this sudden reverse; he stood the picture of disappointment, with crimsoned cheeks, quivering lips, and eyes bent on the floor. His mother, stifling her own mortification, tried to soothe his with the prospect of Miss Osborne's second promise, but though he contrived to utter, with an effort of boyish bravery, 'Oh, I do not mind it!' it was very evident, by the unceasing agitation of his features, that he minded it as much as ever.

Emma did not think or reflect; she felt and acted. 'I shall be very happy to dance with you, sir, if you like it,' said she, holding out her hand with the most unaffected good humour. The boy, in one moment restored to all his first delight, looked joyfully at his mother, and stepping forwards with an honest and simple 'Thank you, ma'am', was instantly ready to attend his new acquaintance. The thankfulness of Mrs Blake was more diffuse; with a look most expressive of unexpected pleasure and lively gratitude, she turned to her neighbour with repeated and fervent acknowledgments of so great and condescending a kindness to her boy. Emma, with perfect truth, could assure her that she could not be giving greater pleasure than she felt herself, and Charles being provided with his gloves and charged to keep them on, they joined the set that was now rapidly forming, with nearly equal complacency. It was a partnership that could not be noticed without surprise. It gained her a broad stare from Miss Osborne and Miss Carr as they passed her in the dance. 'Upon my word, Charles, you are in luck,' said the former, as she turned him; 'you have got a better partner than me'; to which the happy Charles answered 'Yes'.

Tom Musgrave, who was dancing with Miss Carr, gave her many inquisitive glances, and after a time Lord Osborne himself came, and under pretence of talking to Charles, stood to look at his partner. Though rather distressed by such observation, Emma could not repent what she had done, so happy had it made both the boy and his mother, the latter of whom was continually making opportunities of addressing her with the warmest civility. Her little partner, she found, though bent chiefly on dancing, was not unwilling to speak, when her questions or remarks gave him anything to say, and she learnt, by a sort of inevitable enquiry, that he had two brothers and a sister, that they and their mamma all lived with his uncle at Wickstead, that his uncle taught him Latin, that he was very fond of riding, and had a horse of his own given him by Lord Osborne, and that he had been out once already with Lord Osborne's hounds.

At the end of these dances, Emma found they were to drink tea; Miss Edwards gave her a caution to be at hand, in a manner that convinced her of Mrs Edwards' holding it very important to have them both close to her when she moved into the tea room; and Emma was accordingly on the alert to gain her proper station. It was always the pleasure of the company to have a little bustle and crowd when they adjourned for refreshment. The tea room was a small room within the card room, and in passing through the latter, where the passage was straitened by tables, Mrs Edwards and her party were for a few moments hemmed in. It happened close by Lady Osborne's cassino table; Mr Howard, who belonged to it, spoke to his nephew, and Emma, on perceiving herself the object of attention both to Lady Osborne and him, had just turned away her eyes in time to avoid seeming to hear her young companion delightedly whisper aloud, 'Oh, uncle! do look at my partner; she is so pretty!' As they were immediately in motion again, however, Charles was hurried off without being able to receive his uncle's suffrage. On entering the tea room, in which two long tables were prepared, Lord Osborne was to be seen quite alone at the end of one, as if retreating as far as he could from the ball, to enjoy his own thoughts and gape without restraint. Charles instantly pointed him out to Emma. 'There's Lord Osborne; let you and I go and sit by him.'

'No, no,' said Emma, laughing; 'you must sit with my friends.'

Charles was now free enough to hazard a few questions in his turn. 'What o'clock was it?'

'Eleven.'

'Eleven! and I am not at all sleepy. Mamma said I should be asleep before ten. Do you think Miss Osborne will keep her word with me, when tea is over?'

'Oh, yes! I suppose so'; though she felt that she had no better reason to give than that Miss Osborne had *not* kept it before.

'When shall you come to Osborne Castle?'

'Never, probably. I am not acquainted with the family.'

'But you may come to Wickstead and see mamma, and she can take you to the castle. There is a monstrous curious stuffed fox there, and a badger; anybody would think they were alive. It is a pity you should not see them.'

On rising from tea, there was again a scramble for the pleasure of being first out of the room, which happened to be increased by one or two of the card-parties having just broken up, and the players being disposed to move exactly the different way. Among these was Mr Howard, his sister leaning on his arm, and no sooner were they within reach of Emma, than Mrs Blake, calling her notice by a friendly touch, said, 'Your goodness to Charles, my dear Miss Watson, brings all his family upon you. Give me leave to introduce my brother, Mr Howard.' Emma curtsied, the gentleman bowed, made a hasty request for the honour of her hand in the two next dances, to which as hasty an affirmative was given, and they were immediately impelled in opposite directions. Emma was very well pleased with the circumstance; there was a quietly cheerful, gentlemanlike air in Mr Howard that suited her, and in a few minutes afterwards the value of her engagement increased, when, as she was sitting in the card room, somewhat screened by a door, she heard Lord Osborne, who was lounging on a vacant table near her, call Tom Musgrave towards him and say, 'Why do not you dance with that beautiful Emma Watson? I want you to dance with her, and I will come and stand by you.'

'I was determining on it this very moment, my lord; I'll be introduced and dance with her directly.'

'Aye, do, and if you find she does not want much talking to, you may introduce me by and by.'

'Very well, my lord; if she is like her sisters, she will only want to be listened to. I will go this moment. I shall find her in the tea room. That stiff old Mrs Edwards has never done tea.'

Away he went, Lord Osborne after him, and Emma lost no time in hurrying from her corner exactly the other way, forgetting in her haste that she left Mrs Edwards behind.

'We had quite lost you,' said Mrs Edwards, who followed her with Mary in less than five minutes. 'If you prefer this room to the other, there is no reason why you should not be here, but we had better all be together.'

Emma was saved the trouble of apologising, by their being joined at the moment by Tom Musgrave, who requesting Mrs Edwards aloud to do him the honour of presenting him to Miss Emma Watson, left that good lady without any choice in the business, but that of testifying by the coldness of her manner that she did it unwillingly. The honour of dancing with her was solicited without loss of time, and Emma, however she might like to be thought a beautiful girl by lord or commoner, was so little disposed to favour Tom Musgrave himself that she had considerable satisfaction in avowing her previous engagement. He was evidently surprised and discomposed. The style of her last partner had probably led him to believe her not overpowered with applications.

'My little friend Charles Blake,' he cried, 'must not expect to engross you the whole evening. We can never suffer this. It is against the rules of the assembly, and I am sure it will never be patronised by our good friend here, Mrs Edwards; she is by much too nice a judge of decorum to give her licence to such a dangerous particularity – '

'I am not going to dance with Master Blake, sir!'

The gentleman, a little disconcerted, could only hope he might be fortunate another time, and seeming unwilling to leave her, though his friend Lord Osborne was waiting in the doorway for the result, as Emma with some amusement perceived, he began to make civil enquiries after her family.

'How comes it that we have not the pleasure of seeing your sisters here this evening? Our assemblies have been used to be so well treated by them that we do not know how to take this neglect.'

'My eldest sister is the only one at home, and she could not leave my father.'

'Miss Watson the only one at home! You astonish me! It seems but the day before yesterday that I saw them all three in this town. But I am afraid I have been a very sad neighbour of late. I hear dreadful complaints of my negligence wherever I go, and I confess it is a shameful length of time since I was at Stanton. But I shall *now* endeavour to make myself amends for the past.'

Emma's calm courtesy in reply must have struck him as very unlike the encouraging warmth he had been used to receive from her sisters, and gave him probably the novel sensation of doubting his own influence, and of wishing for more attention than she bestowed. The dancing now recommenced; Miss Carr being impatient to *call*, everybody was required to stand up, and Tom Musgrave's curiosity was appeased on seeing Mr Howard come forward and claim Emma's hand.

'That will do as well for me,' was Lord Osborne's remark, when his friend carried him the news, and he was continually at Howard's elbow during the two dances.

The frequency of his appearance there was the only unpleasant part of the engagement, the only objection she could make to Mr Howard. In himself, she thought him as agreeable as he looked, though chatting on the commonest topics, he had a sensible, unaffected way of expressing himself, which made them all worth hearing, and she only regretted that he had not been able to make his pupil's manners as unexceptionable as his own. The two dances seemed very short, and she had her partner's authority for considering them so. At their conclusion the Osbornes and their train were all on the move.

'We are off at last,' said his lordship to Tom. 'How much longer do *you* stay in this heavenly place – till sunrise?'

'No, faith! my lord; I have had quite enough of it. I assure you, I shall not show myself here again when I have had the honour of attending Lady Osborne to her carriage. I shall retreat in as much secrecy as possible to the most remote corner of the house, where I shall order a barrel of oysters, and be famously snug.'

'Let me see you soon at the castle, and bring me word how she looks by daylight.'

Emma and Mrs Blake parted as old acquaintance, and Charles shook her by the hand, and wished her 'goodbye' at least a dozen times. From Miss Osborne and Miss Carr she received something like a jerking curtsy as they passed her; even Lady Osborne gave her a look of complacency, and his lordship actually came back, after the others were out of the room, to 'beg her pardon', and look in the window seat behind her for the gloves that were visibly compressed in his hand. As Tom Musgrave was seen no more, we may suppose his plan to have succeeded, and imagine him mortifying with his barrel of oysters in dreary solitude, or gladly assisting the landlady in her bar to make fresh negus for the happy dancers above. Emma could not help missing the party by whom she had been, though in some respects unpleasantly, distinguished, and the two dances that followed and concluded the ball were rather flat in comparison with the others. Mr Edwards having played with good luck, they were some of the last in the room.

'Here we are back again, I declare,' said Emma, sorrowfully, as she walked into the dining room, where the table was prepared, and the neat upper maid was lighting the candles. 'My dear Miss Edwards, how soon it is at an end! I wish it could all come over again.'

A great deal of kind pleasure was expressed in her having enjoyed the evening so much, and Mr Edwards was as warm as herself in the praise of the fullness, brilliancy, and spirit of the meeting, though as he had been fixed the whole time at the same table in the same room, with only one change of chairs, it might have seemed a matter scarcely perceived; but he had won four rubbers out of five, and everything went well. His daughter felt the advantage of this gratified state of mind, in the course of the remarks and retrospections that now ensued over the welcome soup.

'How came you not to dance with either of the Mr Tomlinsons, Mary?' said her mother.

'I was always engaged when they asked me.'

'I thought you were to have stood up with Mr James the two last dances; Mrs Tomlinson told me he was gone to ask you, and I had heard you say two minutes before that you were *not* engaged.'

'Yes, but there was a mistake; I had misunderstood. I did not know I was engaged. I thought it had been for the two dances after, if we stayed so long, but Captain Hunter assured me it was for those very two.'

'So you ended with Captain Hunter, Mary, did you?' said her father. 'And whom did you begin with?'

'Captain Hunter,' was repeated in a very humble tone.

'Hum! That is being constant, however. But who else did you dance with?'

'Mr Norton and Mr Styles.'

'And who are they?'

'Mr Norton is a cousin of Captain Hunter's.'

'And who is Mr Styles?'

'One of his particular friends.'

'All in the same regiment,' added Mrs Edwards. 'Mary was surrounded by redcoats all the evening. I should have been better pleased to see her dancing with some of our old neighbours, I confess.'

'Yes, yes; we must not neglect our old neighbours. But if these soldiers are quicker than other people in a ballroom, what are young ladies to do?'

'I think there is no occasion for their engaging themselves so many dances beforehand, Mr Edwards.'

'No, perhaps not, but I remember, my dear, when you and I did the same.'

Mrs Edwards said no more, and Mary breathed again. A good deal of good-humoured pleasantry followed, and Emma went to bed in charming spirits, her head full of Osbornes, Blakes, and Howards.

The next morning brought a great many visitors. It was the way of the place always to call on Mrs Edwards the morning after a ball, and this neighbourly inclination was increased in the present instance by a general spirit of curiosity on Emma's account, as everybody wanted to look again at the girl who had been admired the night before by Lord Osborne. Many were the eyes, and various the degrees of approbation with which she was examined. Some saw no fault, and some no beauty. With some her brown skin was the annihilation of every grace, and others could never be persuaded that she was half so handsome as Elizabeth Watson had been ten years ago. The morning passed quickly away in discussing the merits of the ball with all this succession of company, and Emma was at once astonished by finding it two o'clock, and considering that she had heard nothing of her father's chair. After this discovery, she had walked twice to the window to examine the street, and was on the point of asking leave to ring the bell and make enquiries, when the light sound of a carriage driving up to the door set her heart at ease. She stepped again to the window, but instead of the convenient though very un-smart family equipage, perceived a neat curricle. Mr Musgrave was shortly afterwards announced, and Mrs Edwards put on her very stiffest look at the sound. Not at all dismayed, however, by her chilling air, he paid his compliments to each of the ladies with no unbecoming ease, and continuing to address Emma, presented her a note, which 'he had the honour of bringing from her sister, but to which he must observe a verbal post-script from himself would be requisite.'

The note, which Emma was beginning to read rather *before* Mrs Edwards had entreated her to use no ceremony, contained a few lines from Elizabeth importing that their father, in consequence of being unusually well, had taken the sudden resolution of attending the visitation that day, and that as his road lay quite wide from D—, it was impossible for her to come home till the following morning, unless the Edwardses would send her, which was hardly to be expected, or she could meet with any chance conveyance, or did not mind walking so far. She had scarcely run her eye through the whole, before she found herself obliged to listen to Tom Musgrave's further account.

'I received that note from the fair hands of Miss Watson only ten minutes ago,' said he; 'I met her in the village of Stanton, whither my good stars prompted me to turn my horses' heads. She was at that moment in quest of a person to employ on the errand, and I was fortunate enough to convince her that she could not find a more willing or speedy messenger than myself. Remember, I say nothing of my disinterestedness. My reward is to be the indulgence of conveying you to Stanton in my curricle. Though they are not written down, I bring your sister's orders for the same.'

Emma felt distressed; she did not like the proposal – she did not wish to be on terms of intimacy with the proposer; and yet, fearful of encroaching on the Edwardses, as well as wishing to go home herself, she was at a loss how entirely to decline what he offered. Mrs Edwards continued silent, either not understanding the case, or waiting to see how the young lady's inclination lay. Emma thanked him, but professed herself very unwilling to give him so much trouble. 'The trouble was of course honour, pleasure, delight, – what had he or his horses to do?' Still she hesitated – 'She believed she must beg leave to decline his assistance; she was rather afraid of the sort of carriage. The distance was not beyond a walk.' Mrs Edwards was silent no longer. She enquired into the particulars, and then said, 'We shall be extremely happy, Miss Emma, if you can give us the pleasure of your company till tomorrow, but if you cannot conveniently do so, our carriage is quite at your service, and Mary will be pleased with the opportunity of seeing your sister.'

This was precisely what Emma had longed for, and she accepted the offer most thankfully, acknowledging that as Elizabeth was entirely alone, it was her wish to return home to dinner. The plan was warmly opposed by their visitor –

'I cannot suffer it, indeed. I must not be deprived of the happiness of escorting you. I assure you there is not a possibility of fear with my horses. You might guide them yourself. *Your sisters* all know how quiet they are; they have none of them the smallest scruple in trusting themselves with me, even on a racecourse. Believe me,' added he, lowering his voice, '*you* are quite safe – the danger is only *mine*.'

Emma was not more disposed to oblige him for all this.

'And as to Mrs Edwards' carriage being used the day after a ball, it is a thing quite out of rule, I assure you – never heard of before. The old coachman will look as black as his horses – won't he Miss Edwards?'

No notice was taken. The ladies were silently firm, and the gentleman found himself obliged to submit.

'What a famous ball we had last night!' he cried, after a short pause. 'How long did you keep it up after the Osbornes and I went away?'

'We had two dances more.'

'It is making it too much of a fatigue, I think, to stay so late. I suppose your set was not a very full one.'

'Yes; quite as full as ever, except the Osbornes. There seemed no vacancy anywhere, and everybody danced with uncommon spirit to the very last.'

Emma said this, though against her conscience.

'Indeed! perhaps I might have looked in upon you again, if I had been aware of as much, for I am rather fond of dancing than not. Miss Osborne is a charming girl, is not she?'

'I do not think her handsome,' replied Emma, to whom all this was chiefly addressed.

'Perhaps she is not critically handsome, but her manners are delightful. And Fanny Carr is a most interesting little creature. You can imagine nothing more naive or *piquante*; and what do you think of *Lord Osborne*, Miss Watson?'

'He would be handsome even though he were *not* a lord, and perhaps, better bred; more desirous of pleasing and showing himself pleased in a right place.'

'Upon my word, you are severe upon my friend! I assure you Lord Osborne is a very good fellow.'

'I do not dispute his virtues, but I do not like his careless air.'

'If it were not a breach of confidence,' replied Tom, with an important look, 'perhaps I might be able to win a more favourable opinion of poor Osborne.'

Emma gave him no encouragement, and he was obliged to keep his friend's secret. He was also obliged to put an end to his visit, for Mrs Edwards having ordered her carriage, there was no time to be lost on Emma's side in preparing for it. Miss Edwards accompanied her home, but as it was dinner hour at Stanton, stayed with them only a few minutes.

'Now, my dear Emma,' said Miss Watson, as soon as they were alone, 'you must talk to me all the rest of the day without stopping, or I shall not be satisfied, but, first of all, Nanny shall bring in the dinner. Poor thing! You will not dine as you did yesterday, for we have nothing but some fried beef. How nice Mary Edwards looks in her new pelisse! And now tell me how you like them all, and what I am to say to Sam. I have begun my letter, Jack Stokes is to call for it tomorrow, for his uncle is going within a mile of Guildford the next day.'

Nanny brought in the dinner.

'We will wait upon ourselves,' continued Elizabeth, 'and then we shall lose no time. And so, you would not come home with Tom Musgrave?'

'No, you had said so much against him that I could not wish either for the obligation or the intimacy that the use of his carriage must have created. I should not even have liked the appearance of it.'

'You did very right; though I wonder at your forbearance, and I do not think I could have done it myself. He seemed so eager to fetch you that I could not say no, though it rather went against me to be throwing you together, so well as I knew his tricks, but I did long to see you, and it was a clever way of getting you home. Besides, it won't do to be too nice. Nobody could have thought of the Edwardses' letting you have their coach, after the horses being out so late. But what am I to say to Sam?'

'If you are guided by me, you will not encourage him to think of Miss Edwards. The father is decidedly against him, the mother shows him no favour, and I doubt his having any interest with Mary. She danced twice with Captain Hunter, and I think shows him in general as much encouragement as is consistent with her disposition and the circumstances she is placed in. She once mentioned Sam, and certainly with a little confusion, but that was perhaps merely owing to the consciousness of his liking her, which may very probably have come to her knowledge.'

'Oh, dear! yes. She has heard enough of that from us all. Poor Sam! he is out of luck as well as other people. For the life of me, Emma, I cannot help feeling for those that are crossed in love. Well, now begin, and give me an account of everything as it happened.'

Emma obeyed her, and Elizabeth listened with very little interruption till she heard of Mr Howard as a partner.

'Dance with Mr Howard! Good heavens! you don't say so! Why, he is quite one of the great and grand ones. Did you not find him very high?'

'His manners are of a kind to give *me* much more ease and confidence than Tom Musgrave's.'

'Well, go on. I should have been frightened out of my wits to have had anything to do with the Osbornes' set.'

Emma concluded her narration.

'And so you really did not dance with Tom Musgrave at all, but you must have liked him, – you must have been struck with him altogether.'

'I do *not* like him, Elizabeth. I allow his person and air to be good, and that his manners to a certain point – his address rather – is pleasing, but I see nothing else to admire in him. On the contrary, he seems very vain, very conceited, absurdly anxious for distinction, and absolutely contemptible in some of the measures he takes for becoming so. There is a ridiculousness about him that entertains me, but his company gives me no other agreeable emotion.'

'My dearest Emma! You are like nobody else in the world. It is well Margaret is not by. You do not offend *me*, though

I hardly know how to believe you, but Margaret would never forgive such words.'

'I wish Margaret could have heard him profess his ignorance of her being out of the country; he declared it seemed only two days since he had seen her.'

'Aye, that is just like him; and yet this is the man she *will* fancy so desperately in love with her. He is no favourite of mine, as you well know, Emma, but you must think him agreeable. Can you lay your hand on your heart, and say you do not?'

'Indeed, I can, both hands, and spread to their widest extent.'

'I should like to know the man you *do* think agreeable.'

'His name is Howard.'

'Howard! Dear me; I cannot think of *him* but as playing cards with Lady Osborne, and looking proud. I must own, however, that it *is* a relief to me to find you can speak as you do of Tom Musgrave. My heart did misgive me that you would like him too well. You talked so stoutly beforehand, that I was sadly afraid your brag would be punished. I only hope it will last, and that he will not come on to pay you much attention. It is a hard thing for a woman to stand against the flattering ways of a man, when he is bent upon pleasing her.'

As their quietly sociable little meal concluded, Miss Watson could not help observing how comfortably it had passed.

'It is so delightful to me,' said she, 'to have things going on in peace and good humour. Nobody can tell how much I hate quarrelling. Now, though we have had nothing but fried beef, how good it has all seemed! I wish everybody were as easily satisfied as you, but poor Margaret is very snappish, and Penelope owns she had rather have quarrelling going on than nothing at all.'

Mr Watson returned in the evening not the worse for the exertion of the day, and, consequently, pleased with what he had done, and glad to talk of it over his own fireside. Emma had not foreseen any interest to herself in the occurrences of a visitation, but when she heard Mr Howard spoken of as the preacher, and as having given them an excellent sermon, she could not help listening with a quicker ear.

'I do not know when I have heard a discourse more to my mind,' continued Mr Watson, 'or one better delivered. He reads extremely well, with great propriety, and in a very impressive manner, and at the same time without any theatrical grimace or violence. I own I do not like much action in the pulpit; I do not like the studied air and artificial inflexions of voice that your very popular and most admired preachers generally have. A simple delivery is much better calculated to inspire devotion, and shows a much better taste. Mr Howard read like a scholar and a gentleman.'

'And what had you for dinner, sir?' said his eldest daughter.

He related the dishes, and told what he had ate himself.

'Upon the whole,' he added, 'I have had a very comfortable day. My old friends were quite surprised to see me amongst them, and I must say that everybody paid me great attention, and seemed to feel for me as an invalid. They would make me sit near the fire, and as the partridges were pretty high, Dr Richards would have them sent away to the other end of the table, "that they might not offend Mr Watson," which I thought very kind of him. But what pleased me as much as anything was Mr Howard's attention. There is a pretty steep flight of steps up to the room we dine in, which do not quite agree with my gouty foot, and Mr Howard walked by me from the bottom to the top, and would make me take his arm. It struck me as very becoming in so young a man, but I am sure

I had no claim to expect it, for I never saw him before in my life. By the by, he enquired after one of my daughters, but I do not know which. I suppose you know among yourselves.'

On the third day after the ball, as Nanny, at five minutes before three, was beginning to bustle into the parlour with the tray and the knife case, she was suddenly called to the front door by the sound of as smart a rap as the end of a riding whip could give, and though charged by Miss Watson to let nobody in, returned in half a minute with a look of awkward dismay to hold the parlour door open for Lord Osborne and Tom Musgrave. The surprise of the young ladies may be imagined. No visitors would have been welcome at such a moment, but such visitors as these – such a one as Lord Osborne at least, a nobleman and a stranger – was really distressing.

He looked a little embarrassed himself, as, on being introduced by his easy, voluble friend, he muttered something of doing himself the honour of waiting upon Mr Watson. Though Emma could not but take the compliment of the visit to herself, she was very far from enjoying it. She felt all the inconsistency of such an acquaintance with the very humble style in which they were obliged to live, and having in her aunt's family been used to many of the elegancies of life, was fully sensible of all that must be open to the ridicule of richer people in her present home. Of the pain of such feelings, Elizabeth knew very little. Her simple mind, or juster reason, saved her from such mortification, and though shrinking under a general sense of inferiority, she felt no particular shame. Mr Watson, as the gentlemen had already heard from Nanny, was not well enough to be downstairs. With much concern they took their seats; Lord Osborne near Emma, and the convenient Mr Musgrave, in high spirits at his own importance, on the other side of the fireplace, with Elizabeth. *He* was at no loss for words, but when Lord Osborne had hoped that Emma had not caught cold at the ball, he had nothing more to say for some time, and could only gratify his eye by occasional glances at his fair neighbour. Emma was not inclined to give herself much trouble for his entertainment, and after hard labour of mind, he produced the remark of its being a very fine day, and followed it up with the question of, 'Have you been walking this morning?'

'No, my lord; we thought it too dirty.'

'You should wear half-boots.' After another pause: 'Nothing sets off a neat ankle more than a half-boot; nankeen galoshes with black looks very well. Do not you like half-boots?'

'Yes, but unless they are so stout as to injure their beauty, they are not fit for country walking.'

'Ladies should ride in dirty weather. Do you ride?'

'No, my lord.'

'I wonder every lady does not; a woman never looks better than on horseback.'

'But every woman may not have the inclination, or the means.'

'If they knew how much it became them, they would all have the inclination, and I fancy, Miss Watson, when once they had the inclination, the means would soon follow.'

'Your lordship thinks we always have our own way. *That* is a point on which ladies and gentlemen have long disagreed, but without pretending to decide it, I may say that there are some circumstances that even *women* cannot control. Female economy will do a great deal my lord: but it cannot turn a small income into a large one.'

Lord Osborne was silenced. Her manner had been neither sententious nor sarcastic, but there was a something in its mild seriousness, as well as in the words themselves, that made his lordship think, and when he addressed her again, it was with a degree of considerate propriety totally unlike the half-awkward, half-fearless style of his former remarks. It was a new thing with him to wish to please a woman; it was the first time that he had ever felt what was due to a woman in Emma's situation; but as he wanted neither in sense nor a good disposition, he did not feel it without effect.

'You have not been long in this country, I understand,' said he, in the tone of a gentleman. 'I hope you are pleased with it.'

He was rewarded by a gracious answer, and a more liberal full view of her face than she had yet bestowed. Unused to exert himself, and happy in contemplating her, he then sat in silence for some minutes longer, while Tom Musgrave was chattering to Elizabeth, till they were interrupted by Nanny's approach, who, half-opening the door and putting in her head, said –

'Please, ma'am, master wants to know why he ben't to have his dinner?'

The gentlemen, who had hitherto disregarded every symptom, however positive, of the nearness of that meal, now jumped up with apologies, while Elizabeth called briskly after Nanny 'to tell Betty to take up the fowls'.

'I am sorry it happens so,' she added, turning good-humouredly towards Musgrave, 'but you know what early hours we keep.'

Tom had nothing to say for himself; he knew it very well, and such honest simplicity, such shameless truth, rather bewildered him. Lord Osborne's parting compliments took some time, his inclination for speech seeming to increase with the shortness of the term for indulgence. He recommended exercise in defiance of dirt; spoke again in praise of half-boots; begged that his sister might be allowed to send Emma the name of her shoemaker; and concluded with saying, 'My hounds will be hunting this country next week. I believe they will throw off at Stanton Wood on Wednesday at nine o'clock. I mention this in hopes of your being drawn out to see what's going on. If the morning's tolerable, pray do us the honour of giving us your good wishes in person.'

The sisters looked on each other with astonishment when their visitors had withdrawn.

'Here's an unaccountable honour!' cried Elizabeth, at last. 'Who would have thought of Lord Osborne's coming to Stanton? He is very handsome, but Tom Musgrave looks all to nothing the smartest and most fashionable man of the two. I am glad he did not say anything to me; I would not have had to talk to such a great man for the world. Tom was very agreeable, was not he? But did you hear him ask where Miss Penelope and Miss Margaret were, when he first came in? It put me out of patience. I am glad Nanny had not laid the cloth, however – it would have looked so awkward; just the tray did not signify.' To say that Emma was not flattered by Lord Osborne's visit would be to assert a very unlikely thing, and describe a very odd young lady, but the gratification was by no means unalloyed: his coming was a sort of notice that might please her vanity, but did not suit her pride, and she would rather have known that he wished the visit without presuming to make it, than have seen him at Stanton.

Among other unsatisfactory feelings, it once occurred to her to wonder why Mr Howard had not taken the same privilege of coming, and accompanied his lordship, but she was willing to suppose that he had either known nothing about it, or had declined any share in a measure that carried quite as much impertinence in its form as good breeding. Mr Watson was very far from being delighted when he heard what had passed; a little peevish under immediate pain, and ill-disposed to be pleased, he only replied –

'Phoo! phoo! what occasion could there be for Lord Osborne's coming? I have lived here fourteen years without being noticed by any of the family. It is some foolery of that idle fellow, Tom Musgrave. I cannot return the visit. *I* would not if I could.' And when Tom Musgrave was met with again, he was commissioned with a message of excuse to Osborne Castle, on the too-sufficient plea of Mr Watson's infirm state of health.

A week or ten days rolled quietly away after this visit before any new bustle arose to interrupt even for half a day the tranquil and affectionate intercourse of the two sisters, whose mutual regard was increasing with the intimate knowledge of each other that such intercourse produced. The first circumstance to break in on this security was the receipt of a letter from Croydon to announce the speedy return of Margaret, and a visit of two or three days from Mr and Mrs Robert Watson, who undertook to bring her home, and wished to see their sister Emma.

It was an expectation to fill the thoughts of the sisters at Stanton, and to busy the hours of one of them at least, for as Jane had been a woman of fortune, the preparations for her entertainment were considerable, and as Elizabeth had at all times more goodwill than method in her guidance of the house, she could make no change without a bustle. An absence of fourteen years had made all her brothers and sisters strangers to Emma, but in her expectation of Margaret there was more than the awkwardness of such an alienation; she had heard things that made her dread her return, and the day that brought the party to Stanton seemed to her the probable conclusion of almost all that had been comfortable in the house.

Robert Watson was an attorney at Croydon, in a good way of business; very well satisfied with himself for the same, and for having married the only daughter of the attorney to whom he had been clerk, with a fortune of six thousand pounds. Mrs Robert was not less pleased with herself for having had that six thousand pounds, and for being now in possession of a very smart house in Croydon, where she gave genteel parties and wore fine clothes. In her person there was nothing remarkable; her manners were pert and conceited. Margaret was not without beauty; she had a slight pretty figure, and rather wanted countenance than good features, but the sharp and anxious expression of her face made her beauty in general little felt. On meeting her long-absent sister, as on every occasion of show, her manner was all affection and her voice all gentleness; continual smiles and a very slow articulation being her constant resource when determined on pleasing.

She was now so 'delighted to see dear, dear Emma,' that she could hardly speak a word in a minute.

'I am sure we shall be great friends,' she observed with much sentiment, as they were sitting together. Emma scarcely knew how to answer such a proposition, and the manner in which it was spoken she could not attempt to equal. Mrs Robert Watson eyed her with much familiar curiosity and triumphant compassion: the loss of the aunt's fortune was uppermost in her mind at the moment of meeting, and she could not but feel how much better it was to be the daughter of a gentleman of property in Croydon than the niece of an old woman who threw herself away on an Irish captain. Robert was carelessly kind, as became a prosperous man and a brother, more intent on settling with the postboy, inveighing against the exorbitant advance in posting, and pondering over a doubtful half-crown, than on welcoming a sister who was no longer likely to have any property for him to get the direction of.

'Your road through the village is infamous, Elizabeth,' said he; 'worse than ever it was. By Heaven! I would indict it if I lived near you. Who is surveyor now?'

There was a little niece at Croydon to be fondly enquired after by the kind-hearted Elizabeth, who regretted very much her not being of the party.

'You are very good,' replied her mother, 'and I assure you it went very hard with Augusta to have us come away without her. I was forced to say we were only going to church, and promise to come back for her directly. But you know it would not do to bring her without her maid, and I am as particular as ever in having her properly attended to.'

'Sweet little darling!' cried Margaret. 'It quite broke my heart to leave her.'

'Then why was you in such a hurry to run away from her?' cried Mrs Robert. 'You are a sad, shabby girl. I have been quarrelling with you all the way we came, have not I? Such a visit as this, I never heard of! You know how glad we are to have any of you with us, if it be for months together; and I am sorry' (with a witty smile) 'we have not been able to make Croydon agreeable this autumn.'

'My dearest Jane, do not overpower me with your raillery. You know what inducements I had to bring me home. Spare me, I entreat you. I am no match for your arch sallies.'

'Well, I only beg you will not set your neighbours against the place. Perhaps Emma may be tempted to go back with us and stay till Christmas, if you don't put in your word.'

Emma was greatly obliged. 'I assure you we have very good society at Croydon. I do not much attend the balls, they are rather too mixed, but our parties are very select and good. I had seven tables last week in my drawing room. Are you fond of the country? How do you like Stanton?'

'Very much,' replied Emma, who thought a comprehensive answer most to the purpose. She saw that her sister-in-law despised her immediately. Mrs Robert Watson was indeed wondering what sort of a home Emma could possibly have been used to in Shropshire, and setting it down as certain that the aunt could never have had six thousand pounds.

'How charming Emma is,' whispered Margaret to Mrs Robert, in her most languishing tone. Emma was quite distressed by such behaviour, and she did not like it better when she heard Margaret five minutes afterwards say to Elizabeth in a sharp, quick accent, totally unlike the first, 'Have you heard from Pen since she went to Chichester? I had a letter the other day. I don't find she is likely to make anything of it. I fancy she'll come back "Miss Penelope", as she went.'

Such, she feared, would be Margaret's common voice when the novelty of her own appearance were over; the tone of artificial sensibility was not recommended by the idea. The ladies were invited upstairs to prepare for dinner.

'I hope you will find things tolerably comfortable, Jane,' said Elizabeth, as she opened the door of the spare bedchamber.

'My good creature,' replied Jane, 'use no ceremony with me, I entreat you. I am one of those who always take things as they find them. I hope I can put up with a small apartment for two or three nights without making a piece of work. I always wish to be treated quite *en famille* when I come to see you. And now I do hope you have not been getting a great dinner for us. Remember, we never eat suppers.'

'I suppose,' said Margaret, rather quickly to Emma, 'you and I are to be together; Elizabeth always takes care to have a room to herself.'

'No. Elizabeth gives me half hers.'

'Oh!' in a softened voice, and rather mortified to find that she was not ill-used, 'I am sorry I am not to have the pleasure of your company, especially as it makes me nervous to be much alone.'

Emma was the first of the females in the parlour again; on entering it she found her brother alone.

'So, Emma,' said he, 'you are quite a stranger at home. It must seem odd enough for you to be here. A pretty piece of work your Aunt Turner has made of it! By Heaven! a woman should never be trusted with money. I always said she ought to have settled something on you, as soon as her husband died.'

'But that would have been trusting *me* with money,' replied Emma; 'and *I* am a woman too.'

'It might have been secured to your future use, without your having any power over it now. What a blow it must have been upon you! To find yourself, instead of heiress of 8,000 or 9,000 l., sent back a weight upon your family, without a sixpence. I hope the old woman will smart for it.'

'Do not speak disrespectfully of her; she was very good to me, and if she has made an imprudent choice, she will suffer more from it herself than *I* can possibly do.'

'I do not mean to distress you, but you know everybody must think her an old fool. I thought Turner had been reckoned an extraordinarily sensible, clever man. How the devil came he to make such a will?'

'My uncle's sense is not at all impeached in my opinion by his attachment to my aunt. She had been an excellent wife to him. The most liberal and enlightened minds are always the most confiding. The event has been unfortunate, but my uncle's memory is, if possible, endeared to me by such a proof of tender respect for my aunt.'

'That's odd sort of talking. He might have provided decently for his widow, without leaving everything that he had to dispose of, or any part of it, at her mercy.'

'My aunt may have erred,' said Emma, warmly; 'she *has* erred, but my uncle's conduct was faultless. I was her own niece, and he left to herself the power and the pleasure of providing for me.'

'But unluckily she has left the pleasure of providing for you to your father, and without the power. That's the long and short of the business. After keeping you at a distance from your family for such a length of time as must do away all natural affection among us, and breeding you up (I suppose) in a superior style, you are returned upon their hands without a sixpence.'

'You know,' replied Emma, struggling with her tears, 'my uncle's melancholy state of health. He was a greater invalid than my father. He could not leave home.'

'I do not mean to make you cry,' said Robert, rather softened – and after a short silence, by way of changing the subject, he added: 'I am just come from my father's room; he seems very indifferent. It will be a sad break up when he dies. Pity you can none of you get married! You must come to Croydon as well as the rest, and see what you can do there. I believe if Margaret had had a thousand or fifteen hundred pounds, there was a young man who would have thought of her.'

Emma was glad when they were joined by the others; it was better to look at her sister-in-law's finery than listen to Robert, who had equally irritated and grieved her. Mrs Robert, exactly as smart as she had been at her own party, came in with apologies for her dress.

'I would not make you wait,' said she; 'so I put on the first thing I met with. I am afraid I am a sad figure. My dear Mr W.,' (to her husband) 'you have not put any fresh powder in your hair.'

'No, I do not intend it. I think there is powder enough in my hair for my wife and sisters.'

'Indeed, you ought to make some alteration in your dress before dinner when you are out visiting, though you do not at home.'

'Nonsense.'

'It is very odd you should not like to do what other gentlemen do. Mr Marshall and Mr Hemmings change their dress every day of their lives before dinner. And what was the use of my putting up your last new coat, if you are never to wear it?'

'Do be satisfied with being fine yourself, and leave your husband alone.'

To put an end to this altercation and soften the evident vexation of her sister-in-law, Emma (though in no spirits to make such nonsense easy) began to admire her gown. It produced immediate complacency.

'Do you like it?' said she. 'I am very happy. It has been excessively admired, but sometimes I think the pattern too large. I shall wear one tomorrow that I think you will prefer to this. Have you seen the one I gave Margaret?'

Dinner came, and except when Mrs Robert looked at her husband's head, she continued gay and flippant, chiding Elizabeth for the profusion on the table, and absolutely protesting against the entrance of the roast turkey, which formed the only exception to 'You see your dinner'. 'I do beg and entreat that no turkey may be seen today. I am really frightened out of my wits with the number of dishes we have already. Let us have no turkey, I beseech you.'

'My dear,' replied Elizabeth, 'the turkey is roasted, and it may just as well come in as stay in the kitchen. Besides, if it is cut, I am in hopes my father may be tempted to eat a bit, for it is rather a favourite dish.'

'You may have it in, my dear, but I assure you I shan't touch it.'

Mr Watson had not been well enough to join the party at dinner, but was prevailed on to come down and drink tea with them.

'I wish we may be able to have a game of cards tonight,' said Elizabeth to Mrs Robert, after seeing her father comfortably seated in his armchair.

'Not on my account, my dear, I beg. You know I am no card-player. I think a snug chat infinitely better. I always say cards are very well sometimes to break a formal circle, but one never wants them among friends.'

'I was thinking of its being something to amuse my father,' said Elizabeth, 'if it was not disagreeable to you. He says his head won't bear whist, but perhaps if we make a round game he may be tempted to sit down with us.'

'By all means, my dear creature. I am quite at your service; only do not oblige me to choose the game, that's all. *Speculation* is the only round game at Croydon now, but I can play anything. When there is only one or two of you at home, you must be quite at a loss to amuse him. Why do you not get him to play at cribbage? Margaret and I have played at cribbage most nights that we have not been engaged.'

A sound like a distant carriage was at this moment caught; everybody listened; it became more decided; it certainly drew nearer. It was an unusual sound for Stanton at any time of the day, for the village was on no very public road, and contained no gentleman's family but the rector's. The wheels rapidly approached; in two minutes the general expectation was answered; they stopped beyond a doubt at the garden gate of the parsonage. 'Who could it be? It was certainly a post-chaise. Penelope was the only creature to be thought of; she might perhaps have met with some unexpected opportunity of returning.' A pause of suspense ensued. Steps were distinguished along the paved footway, which led under the windows of the house to the front door, and then within the passage. They were the steps of a man. It could not be Penelope. It must be Samuel. The door opened, and displayed Tom Musgrave in the wrap of a traveller. He had been in London, and was now on his way home, and he had come half a mile out of his road merely to call for ten minutes at Stanton. He loved to take people by surprise with sudden visits at extraordinary seasons, and, in the present instance, had had the additional motive of being able to tell the Miss Watsons, whom he depended on finding sitting quietly employed after tea, that he was going home to an eight o'clock dinner.

As it happened, however, he did not give more surprise than he received, when, instead of being shown into the usual little sitting room, the door of the best parlour (a foot larger each way than the other) was thrown open, and he beheld a circle of smart people whom he could not immediately recognise arranged, with all the honours of visiting, round the fire, and Miss Watson seated at the best Pembroke table, with the best tea-things before her. He stood a few seconds in silent amazement. 'Musgrave!' ejaculated Margaret, in a tender voice. He recollected himself, and came forward, delighted to find such a circle of friends, and blessing his good fortune for the unlooked-for indulgence. He shook hands with Robert, bowed and smiled to the ladies, and did everything very prettily, but as to any particularity of address or emotion towards Margaret, Emma, who closely observed him, per-ceived nothing that did not justify Elizabeth's opinion, though Margaret's modest smiles imported that she meant to take the visit to herself. He was persuaded without much difficulty to throw off his greatcoat and drink tea with them. For 'whether he dined at eight or nine,' as he observed, 'was a matter of very little consequence'; and without seeming to seek, he did not turn away from the chair close by Margaret, which she was assiduous in providing him. She had thus secured him from her sisters, but it was not immediately in her power to preserve him from her brother's claims, for as he came avowedly from London, and had left it only four hours ago, the last current report as to public news, and the general opinion of the day, must be understood before Robert could let his attention be yielded to the less national and important demands of the women. At last, however, he was at liberty to hear Margaret's soft address, as she spoke her fears of his having had a most terrible cold, dark, dreadful journey.

'Indeed, you should not have set out so late.'

'I could not be earlier,' he replied. 'I was detained chatting at the Bedford by a friend. All hours are alike to me. How long have you been in the country, Miss Margaret?'

'We only came this morning; my kind brother and sister brought me home this very morning. 'Tis singular, is not it?'

'You were gone a great while, were not you? A fortnight, I suppose?'

'*You* may call a fortnight a great while, Mr Musgrave,' said Mrs Robert, sharply; 'but *we* think a month very little. I assure you we bring her home at the end of a month much against our will.'

'A month! Have you really been gone a month? 'Tis amazing how time flies.'

'You may imagine,' said Margaret, in a sort of whisper, 'what are my sensations in finding myself once more at Stanton; you know what a sad visitor I make. And I was so excessively impatient to see Emma; I dreaded the meeting, and at the same time longed for it. Do you not comprehend the sort of feeling?'

'Not at all,' cried he, aloud: 'I could never dread a meeting with Miss Emma Watson – or any of her sisters.'

It was lucky that he added that finish.

'Were you speaking to me?' said Emma, who had caught her own name.

'Not absolutely,' he answered; 'but I was thinking of you, as many at a greater distance are probably doing at this moment. Fine open weather, Miss Emma, charming season for hunting.'

'Emma is delightful, is not she?' whispered Margaret; 'I have found her more than answer my warmest hopes. Did you ever see anything more perfectly beautiful? I think even *you* must be a convert to a brown complexion.'

He hesitated. Margaret was fair herself, and he did not particularly want to compliment her, but Miss Osborne and Miss Carr were likewise fair, and his devotion to them carried the day.

'Your sister's complexion,' said he, at last, 'is as fine as a dark complexion can be, but I still profess my preference of a white skin. You have seen Miss Osborne? She is my model for a truly feminine complexion, and she is very fair.'

'Is she fairer than me?'

Tom made no reply. 'Upon my honour, ladies,' said he, giving a glance over his own person, 'I am highly indebted to your condescension for admitting me in such dishabille into your drawing room. I really did not consider how unfit I was to be here, or I hope I should have kept my distance. Lady Osborne would tell me that I were growing as careless as her son, if she saw me in this condition.'

The ladies were not wanting in civil returns, and Robert Watson, stealing a view of his own head in an opposite glass, said with equal civility –

'You cannot be more in dishabille than myself. We got here so late that I had not time even to put a little fresh powder in my hair.'

Emma could not help entering into what she supposed her sister-in-law's feelings at the moment.

When the tea-things were removed, Tom began to talk of his carriage, but the old card table being set out, and the fish and counters, with a tolerably clean pack, brought forward from the buffet by Miss Watson, the general voice was so urgent with him to join their party that he agreed to allow himself another quarter of an hour. Even Emma was pleased that he would stay, for she was beginning to feel that a family party might be the worst of all parties, and the others were delighted.

'What's your game?' cried he, as they stood round the table.

'Speculation, I believe,' said Elizabeth. 'My sister recommends it, and I fancy we all like it. I know *you* do, Tom.'

'It is the only round game played at Croydon now,' said Mrs Robert; 'we never think of any other. I am glad it is a favourite with you.'

'Oh, me!' said Tom. 'Whatever you decide on will be a favourite with *me*. I have had some pleasant hours at speculation in my time, but I have not been in the way of it now for a long while. Vingt-un is the game at Osborne Castle. I have played nothing but vingt-un of late. You would be astonished to hear the noise we make there – the fine old lofty drawing room rings again. Lady Osborne sometimes declares she cannot hear herself speak. Lord Osborne enjoys it famously, and he makes the best dealer without exception that I ever beheld – such quickness and spirit, he lets nobody dream over their cards. I wish you could see him overdraw himself on both his own cards. It is worth anything in the world!'

'Dear me!' cried Margaret, 'why should not we play at vingt-un? I think it is a much better game than speculation. I cannot say I am very fond of speculation.'

Mrs Robert offered not another word in support of the game. She was quite vanquished, and the fashions of Osborne Castle carried it over the fashions of Croydon.

'Do you see much of the parsonage family at the castle, Mr Musgrave?' said Emma, as they were taking their seats.

'Oh, yes; they are almost always there. Mrs Blake is a nice little good-humoured woman; she and I are sworn friends; and Howard's a very gentlemanlike, good sort of fellow! You are not forgotten, I assure you, by any of the party. I fancy you must have a little cheek-glowing now and then, Miss Emma. Were not you rather warm last Saturday about nine or ten o'clock in the evening? I will tell you how it was – I see you are dying to know. Says Howard to Lord Osborne – '

At this interesting moment he was called on by the others to regulate the game, and determine some disputable point, and his attention was so totally engaged in the business, and afterwards by the course of the game, as never to revert to what he had been saying before, and Emma, though suffering a good deal from curiosity, dared not remind him.

He proved a very useful addition to their table. Without him, it would have been a party of such very near relations as could have felt little interest, and perhaps maintained little complaisance, but his presence gave variety and secured good manners. He was, in fact, excellently qualified to shine at a round game, and few situations made him appear to greater advantage. He played with spirit, and had a great deal to say, and, though no wit himself, could sometimes make use of the wit of an absent friend, and had a lively way of retailing a commonplace or saying a mere nothing, that had great effect at a card table. The ways and good jokes of Osborne Castle were now added to his ordinary means of entertainment. He repeated the smart sayings of one lady, detailed the oversights of another, and indulged them even with a copy of Lord Osborne's style of overdrawing himself on both cards.

The clock struck nine while he was thus agreeably occupied, and when Nanny came in with her master's basin of gruel, he had the pleasure of observing to Mr Watson that he should leave him at supper while he went home to dinner himself. The carriage was ordered to the door, and no entreaties for his staying longer could now avail, for he well knew that if he stayed he must sit down to supper in less than ten minutes, which to a man whose heart had been long fixed on calling his next meal a dinner, was quite insupportable. On finding him determined to go, Margaret began to wink and nod at Elizabeth to ask him to dinner for the following day, and Elizabeth at last not able to resist hints that her own hospitable, social temper more than half seconded, gave the invitation: 'Would he give Robert the meeting, they should be very happy?'

'With the greatest pleasure' was his first reply. In a moment afterwards, 'That is, if I can possibly get here in time, but I shoot with Lord Osborne, and therefore must not engage. You will not think of me unless you see me.' And so he departed, delighted with the uncertainty in which he had left it.

Margaret, in the joy of her heart under circumstances that she chose to consider as peculiarly propitious, would willingly have made a confidante of Emma when they were alone for a short time the next morning, and had proceeded so far as to say, 'The young man who was here last night, my dear Emma, and returns today, is more interesting to me than perhaps you may be aware – '; but Emma, pretending to understand nothing extraordinary in the words, made some very inapplicable reply, and jumping up, ran away from a subject that was odious to her feelings. As Margaret would not allow a doubt to be repeated of Musgrave's coming to dinner, preparations were made for his entertainment much exceeding what had been deemed necessary the day before, and taking the office of superintendence entirely from her sister, she was half the morning in the kitchen herself, directing and scolding.

After a great deal of indifferent cooking and anxious suspense, however, they were obliged to sit down without their guest. Tom Musgrave never came, and Margaret was at no pains to conceal her vexation under the disappointment, or repress the peevishness of her temper. The peace of the party for the remainder of that day and the whole of the next, which comprised the length of Robert's and Jane's visit, was continually invaded by her fretful displeasure and querulous attacks. Elizabeth was the usual object of both. Margaret had just respect enough for her brother's and sister's opinion to behave properly by *them*, but Elizabeth and the maids could never do anything right, and Emma, whom she seemed no longer to think about, found the continuance of the gentle voice beyond her calculation short. Eager to be as little among them as possible, Emma was delighted with the alternative of sitting above with her father, and warmly entreated to be his constant companion each evening, and as Elizabeth loved company of any kind too well not to prefer being below at all risks, as she had rather talk of Croydon with Jane, with every interruption of Margaret's perverseness, than sit with only her father, who frequently could not endure talking at all – the affair was so settled, as soon as she could be persuaded to believe it no sacrifice on her sister's part. To Emma, the change was most acceptable and delightful. Her father, if ill, required little more than gentleness and silence, and being a man of sense and education, was, if able to converse, a welcome companion. In *his* chamber Emma was at peace from the dreadful mortifications of unequal society and family discord; from the immediate endurance of hard-hearted prosperity, low-minded conceit, and wrong-headed folly, engrafted on an untoward disposition. She still suffered from them in the contemplation of their existence, in memory and in prospect, but for the moment, she ceased to be tortured by their effects. She was at leisure; she could read and think, though her situation was hardly such as to make reflection very soothing. The evils arising from the loss of her uncle were neither trifling nor likely to lessen, and when thought had been freely indulged, in contrasting the past and the present, the employment of mind and dissipation of unpleasant ideas that only reading could produce made her thankfully turn to a book.

The change in her home, society, and style of life, in consequence of the death of one friend and the imprudence of another, had indeed been striking. From being the first object of hope and solicitude to an uncle who had formed her mind with the care of a parent, and of tenderness to an aunt whose amiable temper had delighted to give her every indulgence; from being the life and spirit of a house where all had been comfort and elegance, and the expected heiress of an easy independence, she was become of importance to no one –

a burden on those whose affections she could not expect, an addition in a house already overstocked, surrounded by inferior minds, with little chance of domestic comfort, and as little hope of future support. It was well for her that she was naturally cheerful, for the change had been such as might have plunged weak spirits in despondence.

She was very much pressed by Robert and Jane to return with them to Croydon, and had some difficulty in getting a refusal accepted, as they thought too highly of their own kindness and situation to suppose the offer could appear in a less advantageous light to anybody else. Elizabeth gave them her interest, though evidently against her own, in privately urging Emma to go.

'You do not know what you refuse, Emma,' said she, 'nor what you have to bear at home. I would advise you by all means to accept the invitation; there is always something lively going on at Croydon. You will be in company almost every day, and Robert and Jane will be very kind to you. As for me, I shall be no worse off without you than I have been used to be, but poor Margaret's disagreeable ways are new to *you*, and they would vex you more than you think for, if you stay at home.'

Emma was of course uninfluenced, except to greater esteem for Elizabeth, by such representations, and the visitors departed without her.

How Jane Austen had intended the *The Watsons* to continue, according to Austen-Leigh's *Memoir*:

When the author's sister, Cassandra, showed the manuscript of this work to some of her nieces, she also told them something of the intended story; for with this dear sister – though, I believe, with no one else – Jane seems to have talked freely of any work that she might have in hand. Mr Watson was soon to die; and Emma to become dependent for a home on her narrow-minded sister-in-law and brother. She was to decline an offer of marriage from Lord Osborne, and much of the interest of the tale was to arise from Lady Osborne's love for Mr Howard, and his counter affection for Emma, whom he was finally to marry.

BIOGRAPHICAL NOTE

Jane Austen was born in 1775 in Steventon, Hampshire, the seventh of eight children. Her father, the Revd George Austen, was a well-read and cultured man, and Jane was mostly educated at home. She read voraciously as a child, in particular the works of Fielding, Sterne, Richardson and Scott. She also began writing at a very young age, producing her earliest work when she was just twelve years old.

Between the writing of *Northanger Abbey* and the revision of *Sense and Sensibility*, Austen wrote *The Watsons*, which she abandoned in 1805, on her father's death, when she and her mother moved to Southampton. They then settled in Chawton, Hampshire, in 1809, and it was here that her major novels were written. Despite leading a remarkably uneventful life herself – she never married, and seldom left home – her works are noted for her incredible powers of observation. Only four novels were published during her lifetime – *Sense and Sensibility* (1811), *Pride and Prejudice* (1813), *Mansfield Park* (1814) and *Emma* (1816) – and all were published anonymously. On a rare visit from home, she was taken ill, and she died from Addison's disease in 1817. Two further novels, *Persuasion* and *Northanger Abbey*, were published post-humously in 1818; *The Watsons* was not published until 1870, as part of James Edward Austen-Leigh's *A Memoir of Jane Austen*. *Sanditon*, the novel she was working on when she died, appeared in 1925.

HESPERUS PRESS CLASSICS

Hesperus Press, as suggested by the Latin motto, is committed to bringing near what is far – far both in space and time. Works written by the greatest authors, and unjustly neglected or simply little known in the English-speaking world, are made accessible through new translations and a completely fresh editorial approach. Through these classic works, the reader is introduced to the greatest writers from all times and all cultures.

For more information on Hesperus Press, please visit our website: **www.hesperuspress.com**

ET REMOTISSIMA PROPE

SELECTED TITLES FROM HESPERUS PRESS

Author	Title	Foreword writer
Pedro Antonio de Alarcón	*The Three-Cornered Hat*	
Louisa May Alcott	*Behind a Mask*	Doris Lessing
Edmondo de Amicis	*Constantinople*	Umberto Eco
Gabriele D'Annunzio	*The Book of the Virgins*	Tim Parks
Pietro Aretino	*The School of Whoredom*	Paul Bailey
Pietro Aretino	*The Secret Life of Nuns*	
Pietro Aretino	*The Secret Life of Wives*	Paul Bailey
Jane Austen	*Lady Susan*	
Jane Austen	*Lesley Castle*	Zoë Heller
Jane Austen	*Love and Friendship*	Fay Weldon
Honoré de Balzac	*Colonel Chabert*	A.N. Wilson
Charles Baudelaire	*On Wine and Hashish*	Margaret Drabble
Aphra Behn	*The Lover's Watch*	
Giovanni Boccaccio	*Life of Dante*	A.N. Wilson
Charlotte Brontë	*The Foundling*	
Charlotte Brontë	*The Green Dwarf*	Libby Purves
Charlotte Brontë	*The Secret*	Salley Vickers
Charlotte Brontë	*The Spell*	Nicola Barker
Emily Brontë	*Poems of Solitude*	Helen Dunmore
Giacomo Casanova	*The Duel*	Tim Parks
Miguel de Cervantes	*The Dialogue of the Dogs*	Ben Okri
Geoffrey Chaucer	*The Parliament of Birds*	
Anton Chekhov	*The Story of a Nobody*	Louis de Bernières
Anton Chekhov	*Three Years*	William Fiennes
Wilkie Collins	*The Frozen Deep*	
Wilkie Collins	*A Rogue's Life*	Peter Ackroyd
Wilkie Collins	*Who Killed Zebedee?*	Martin Jarvis
William Congreve	*Incognita*	Peter Ackroyd

Joseph Conrad	*Heart of Darkness*	A.N. Wilson
Joseph Conrad	*The Return*	Colm Tóibín
James Fenimore Cooper	*Autobiography of a Pocket Handkerchief*	Ruth Scurr
Dante Alighieri	*New Life*	Louis de Bernières
Dante Alighieri	*The Divine Comedy: Inferno*	Ian Thomson
Daniel Defoe	*The King of Pirates*	Peter Ackroyd
Charles Dickens	*The Haunted House*	Peter Ackroyd
Charles Dickens	*A House to Let*	
Charles Dickens	*Mrs Lirriper*	Philip Hensher
Charles Dickens	*Mugby Junction*	Robert Macfarlane
Charles Dickens	*The Wreck of the Golden Mary*	Simon Callow
Emily Dickinson	*The Single Hound*	Andrew Motion
Fyodor Dostoevsky	*The Double*	Jeremy Dyson
Fyodor Dostoevsky	*The Gambler*	Jonathan Franzen
Fyodor Dostoevsky	*Notes from the Underground*	Will Self
Fyodor Dostoevsky	*Poor People*	Charlotte Hobson
Arthur Conan Doyle	*The Mystery of Cloomber*	
Arthur Conan Doyle	*The Tragedy of the Korosko*	Tony Robinson
Alexandre Dumas	*Captain Pamphile*	Tony Robinson
Alexandre Dumas	*One Thousand and One Ghosts*	
Joseph von Eichendorff	*Life of a Good-for-nothing*	
George Eliot	*Amos Barton*	Matthew Sweet
George Eliot	*Mr Gilfil's Love Story*	Kirsty Gunn
J. Meade Falkner	*The Lost Stradivarius*	Tom Paulin
Henry Fielding	*Jonathan Wild the Great*	Peter Ackroyd
Gustave Flaubert	*Memoirs of a Madman*	Germaine Greer
Gustave Flaubert	*November*	Nadine Gordimer
E.M. Forster	*Arctic Summer*	Anita Desai